THIS CANDLEWICK BOOK BELONGS TO:

_____

_____

_____

_____

For all my nieces and nephews • M. L. D.

For Jessica and Cliff • C. A.

To my dear children, Alex, Adam, Jason,
Joshua, Daina, and Dustin. Love, Dad • B. R.

Candlewick Press would like to extend special
thanks to Bruce Raiffe, president of Gund, and
all the staff at Gund for their help and cooperation.

Text copyright © 1995 by Mary Lee Donovan
Illustrations copyright © 1995 by Caroline Anstey
Based on the original character ™SNUFFLES copyright © 1980 by Gund Inc.

First paperback edition 1997

The Library of Congress has cataloged the hardcover edition as follows:

Donovan, Mary Lee.
Snuffles makes a friend / Mary Lee Donovan : illustrated by
Caroline Anstey.—1st ed.
(Gund children's library)
Summary: Snuffles the bear coaxes her bashful neighbor to come out of his shell
and become friends with the other animals by meeting them one at a time.
ISBN 1-56402-497-0 (hardcover)
[1. Bashfulness—Fiction. 2. Bears—Fiction. 3. Friendship—Fiction.
4. Animals—Fiction.] I. Anstey, Caroline, ill. II. Title. III. Series.
PZ7.D7232Sn   1995
[E]—dc20   95-10693

ISBN 0-7636-0096-2 (paperback)

10 9 8 7 6 5 4 3 2 1

Printed in Hong Kong

This book was typeset in Veronan.
The pictures were done in watercolor and pencil.

Candlewick Press
2067 Massachusetts Avenue
Cambridge, Massachusetts 02140

SNUFFLES
MAKES A FRIEND

Mary Lee Donovan   *illustrated by* Caroline Anstey

CANDLEWICK PRESS
CAMBRIDGE, MASSACHUSETTS

SNUFFLES was a bear who always had time for friends and neighbors and a cup of raspberry tea. She loved visitors. Lots of them.

"My house is your house," she said to everyone.

So all the neighbors came to Snuffles's house. All the neighbors, that is, except her new next-door neighbor, Percy. Snuffles didn't know why.

"Why hasn't Percy come to visit?" she asked again and again.

"Maybe he's busy," said Mo.

"Maybe he doesn't like raspberry tea," suggested Roy.

"Maybe he's shy,"
said Jack.
"Oh!" said Snuffles.
"Maybe."

"Maybe you should invite him
over 'specially," said Mo.
"Good idea!" said
Snuffles.

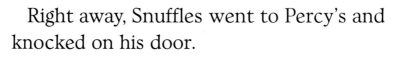

Right away, Snuffles went to Percy's and knocked on his door.

"Hello, neighbor!" she said when Percy answered. "Would you like to come over to my house? Some friends and I are going to listen to music—the complete works of Major Brash and His Marching Band—"

"No, thank you," Percy said, and quietly closed the door.

"Well," Snuffles said to
her friends when she got home,
"marching music *can* be loud if you're
not in the mood for it."

"It's true," they all agreed.

"I'll try again tomorrow," said Snuffles.

The next day, Snuffles went to Percy's
again. *Knock knock knock.*

"Hello, neighbor!" Snuffles said when
Percy opened the door. "Would you like
to come over to my house? Some friends
and I are going to share a caramel cake.
I baked it this morning."

"No, thank you," said Percy, and quietly
closed the door.

"Well," Snuffles said to her friends when she got home, "too many sweets *can* be bad for you."

"It's true," they all agreed.

"I know!" Snuffles said. "I'll have one of my parties. Just for Percy! How could he say no?"

"Good idea," said her friends.

Knock knock knock.

"Hello, neighbor," Snuffles said when
Percy opened the door. "I'm having a party.
There will be games and food and barrels
full of raspberry tea. *Everyone* is invited.
And it's going to be especially for—"

"No, thank you," Percy interrupted,
and quietly closed the door.

"Well," Snuffles said to her friends when she got home, "parties *can* be tiring."

"It's true," they all agreed.

"I'll try again tomorrow." But Snuffles was running out of ideas.

"Sweet potatoes," said Mo.

"Sweet potatoes?" said Snuffles.

"I heard a rumor that Percy likes sweet potatoes. That's what Pru says down at the market."

"Oh!" said Snuffles.

So the next day, Snuffles went to Percy's house again. *Knock knock knock.*

"Hello, neighbor," Snuffles said when Percy opened the door. "Would you like to come over to my house? Some friends and I are going to have a sweet potato festival with lots of sweet potatoes. And lots of people!"

"Lots of people?"

"All the neighbors! All at my place!" said Snuffles.

"No, thank you," said Percy.

Before Percy could close the door, Snuffles cried, "Wait! I want to be your friend, Percy."

"And I want to be your friend, Snuffles," said Percy.

"So why won't you come over to my house?"

"Too many people all at one time. I'm shy."

"I know," said Snuffles.

But neither one of them knew what to do next.

Finally, Percy said, "Snuffles, would you like to come in? I could make us some raspberry tea and a nice sweet potato pie."

"I love raspberry tea!"

"I know," said Percy.

"And a sweet potato pie sounds wonderful!" said Snuffles.

So Snuffles and Percy went inside, just the two of them. They shared a sweet potato pie, drank raspberry tea, and became good friends.

After that, with Snuffles's help, Percy
made friends with all the neighbors—

one neighbor

at a time.

MARY LEE DONOVAN is an editor of children's books as well as an author. She wrote *Snuffles Makes a Friend* to show how making friends often requires "a willingness to try and try again." She adds, "I think a lot of children will sympathize with Percy's feelings." The author of *Papa's Bedtime Story,* Mary Lee Donovan lives in Littleton, Massachusetts.

CAROLINE ANSTEY is the illustrator of numerous children's books, including *Moles Can Dance* by Richard Edwards. "It was a challenge to draw and create a character from a toy. But knowing who I wanted Percy to be helped me to envision the other characters and the setting for this friendly story."